Spilt Milk

Spilt Milk

A Collection of Stories
D.K. Cassidy

ISBN: 978-1941938003

Library of Congress Control Number: 2014913254

Interior Design: NovelNinjutsu.com
Cover Design: Designforwriters.com

Pluvio
press

Contents

Dedication

I dedicate this book to my husband Mark,
my sons Aidan and Jared,
and to my sisters Joan and Fran.

Their love and confidence emboldened me
to step into a new world.

Bee's Knees

They lifted her off the first table and put her on a cold steel platform. Just in case. The nurse transferring all her tubes with a veteran's efficiency. Trying to maintain her dignity by covering the woman's body.

Feel great, she joked. The fast ride through the hospital corridor, the orderly weaving between oncoming groups of people, made her remember amusement rides. He backed into an operating room and stopped next to the table that was to be the new mother's place for the birth of her child.

Like a magician's assistant, body sawed in half, the epidural made her think, Magical! She glanced down to the chilled table, not sure the orderly remembered to transfer her lower half.

Buzzing in her toes alerted the young mother. She wasn't supposed to be feeling anything. The bees crept up her knees. Then she saw panic in her doctor's eyes.

"What's going on? What am I feeling?"

The bees were up to her thighs. The word magical replaced with idiot in her mind. Her body was reconnecting; the magician snapped the box together making her miserably whole. Around her pelvis the bees buzzed furiously. They spread fire. Searing fire, forming a dark cloud around her. Then the tearing and screaming, she called for relief and saw only the staff's apologetic eyes.

"It's too late." one said. "We can't do anything." Several disjointed voices. "It'll be over soon." None of them any help. "Breathe. Breathe. Pant. Pant."

"You breathe. I want off this table. I..." The fire started to die. "It's your fau—"

The bees were replaced, by fluttery moths. They twitched, crowding together.
At last she heaves, moans. Rests. Looking once into the tiny face of her son.

Brief thoughts mixed together in her exhausted mind.

Disappointment. Relief.

No trace of her husband in those brown eyes.

Guilt.

She said her newborn's name once, Caleb. Her eyes flutter. Close. Permanent darkness follows. Her last breath enveloping her new son, an air of desperation marking him.

The agony of withdrawal followed in a few hours; cries of a newborn not understanding his new world of pain. The infant's crying baffled the doctor until she looked at the sparse intake records, not enough information. Heroin, too late she realized what the dead woman was.

The staff in the room quiet, absorbing what just occurred. The anesthesiologist the first to move, pulling on tubing then making notes on his chart. The obstetrician remained still for another minute, thinking what?

Caleb's father sat in the waiting room drinking enhanced vending machine coffee. Johnny Walker. The birth of his child. He wasn't going to drink his usual cheap stuff. He was celebrating. Celebrating with Johnny. Later he'd tell his mother she had a grandson. But first another drink before he visited his wife and the boy.

George

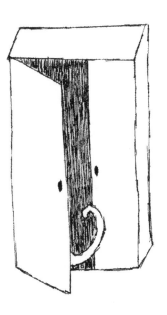

eorge always felt safe in his closet, the only place in the small house that belonged to him. He slept, read, brooded, ate, and sometimes dreamt there. This four-by-six foot world decorated with the things he'd accumulated, was out of bounds for all including his cat.

The previous occupant built a wall of shelves intended to hold whatever a hanger couldn't. His father didn't enter the closet, not out of respect, but neglect. As long as George remained out of his sight, he didn't bother with him. He might walk into George's bedroom looking for the cat, but he never opened the closet door.

On occasion he heard his father walk by but not to seek George. The bathroom stood next to his sanctuary. George blocked out the disturbing sounds of elimination and drunken stumbling by listening to a little clock radio he'd found in someone else's garbage can, humming along to the music.

Five and a half year old George stood in his closet, looking at a book he'd stolen from the library. Learning to read, still a few months away, wasn't a reason to stop taking books. It felt more exciting to take what he wanted, returning the books whenever he got around to it, if ever. The only books to make it back to the library were the ones he tired of.

He'd been doing this for months, the first time without intent. He ran into the library to avoid the rain on his solitary walk home from kindergarten. A colorful book with pictures of dragons on the cover lay on a table near the door. George picked it up and decided he liked these pictures. He wanted to bring the book home.

He had no idea about the system in place to check out items, so he'd stolen the book. Now he had a use for the almost empty backpack he transported to and from school. Later that month, his teacher talked about going on a field trip to the library, getting the class signed up for cards.

George developed a way of blending in, becoming invisible. A book about knights slid into the red backpack at his feet. Instead of feeling guilty he'd taken it, George felt a chill run up his spine, a good chill, something close to happiness. His beleaguered teacher never noticed he stayed away from the desk issuing library cards.

Each year George became interested in a new thing to collect. He discovered plastic army men when he was six years old accompanying his mother to the drugstore, while she picked up her depression medication. While she spoke to the pharmacist, he wandered in a state of boredom through the store. On aisle three he saw a display of cheap plastic toys, designed to entice last minute shoppers, guilty divorced dads, and unsupervised children.

Located on the top shelf sat a round plastic container with the words, "Paratroopers, Complete with Parachutes". Due to his stolen books, George was an excellent reader for his age. He recognized the word parachute. He wasn't certain about the meaning of paratroopers but decided it had to be worth a look.

The toy sat just out of his reach, so he climbed onto the first shelf and grabbed for it. When he looked inside, he discovered his newest passion, army men. He knew this container would be too large to take, so he needled his mother until she relented; she didn't want George to start screaming in the drugstore.

He supplemented his collection with stray army men found on playgrounds, in classmate's backpacks, and smaller packages from local stores that were easier to steal. His armies lined the shelves of his closet and formed groups on top of his books, ready for action.

Eight-year-old George enjoyed counting the battle cards he'd taken as part of his current obsession. He never played the game, but loved to read the powers, abilities, and fight tactics of the illustrated creatures on the decks. Last year's assortment of dump trucks taught him the important lesson of conservation of space. Being practical, he realized collecting smaller items meant room for a more diverse array of objects to hide and display in his world.

Almost every surface of the shelves stood piled high with books, army men, and trucks. He collected thousands of these cards, using up a few inches of space on a stack of books. He was careful to maintain a clear space to lie down and enjoy his collections.

At ten years old, a pillow, some snacks, and his radio turned low, were all George needed to maintain his sense of security. Stockpiled batteries he'd taken on his last trip to the drugstore ensured his radio never stopped playing. The one and only time he couldn't play his radio taught him to stay vigilant about his power sources.

Six months earlier his radio had stopped playing, the batteries dead. George heard the conversation going on in the living room, which in this tiny house was quite close. His father and mother were fighting again. Much of the argument made no sense to him. Then they started making other noises that George hated to hear, noises that made him feel strange and sent chills up his back. Normally his radio hushed the noises nearby. From that day on George always stole batteries.

George's mother, a thin dry woman, doled out her version of love via food. Never hugging George or her late husband. She rarely spoke. Instead choosing to watch television. George would watch TV with her, only if he finished his food. If he disturbed her, he could expect a slap or worse. She'd already dispensed with his father after one of their arguments. George didn't want to disappear. He did what it took to please her.

Soon, George's collection included magazines he discovered at the local convenience store. These publications were out of sight, covered, and in the corner away from the front window. On most days, there were a few older guys milling around flipping through the glossy pages.

One afternoon on the way back from school he noticed no one in that corner. The store clerk busied himself stocking the cups for the self-serve coffee. George headed straight for that corner, picking up the nearest magazine. One glance and he knew he'd discovered his next obsession.

With smooth, practiced motions, the magazine slipped under his jacket. George walked out of the store. That familiar tingling shooting up his spine. Once down the block, he ran home eager to enjoy his new acquisition.

From the dim kitchen, George skipped his typical after school snack, heading straight for his world, shedding his heavy jacket and backpack on the way. He ignored the door, slightly ajar. Turning on the light, he climbed onto his shelf.

He breathed hard from the run, so he didn't hear the sound of his visitor Milky. That cat liked to follow him into the yard then meow until he picked her up. When he was younger, George used to pet and hug Milky until she hissed.

In the closet his hugs kept getting tighter and the petting rougher. The hissing made him mad; he couldn't understand why she didn't enjoy his attention. Today, he kept hugging Milky until she stopped meowing and relaxed. That evening George stole out of his house and deposited a limp Milky in the neighbor's garbage can.

Once the house quieted down, he opened the magazine and stared at the women. The only females he'd seen up close were his teacher, mother, and clerks at the drugstore. None of them looked like this or made him feel funny. He tried to figure out what he felt and knew it to be something good but still quite strange. It was the same feeling he had when his parents used to make noises.

Later that night George decided he wanted to see Milky again. He snuck outside after his mother was asleep and crept into the neighbor's backyard to retrieve his only friend from the garbage can.

D.K. Cassidy

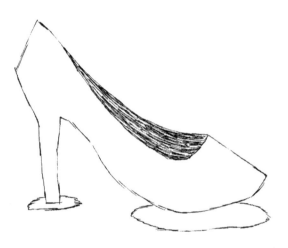

The high court insists I discuss my 'crimes'. Ridiculous. What crimes? I think therapy is not necessary! I was only attempting to be a good mother. My two beautiful daughters needed help getting the attention of the handsome prince. Their annoying stepsister Cinderella constantly thwarted them. Any mother would have acted as I have.

The man in a brown cardigan sat before her, not what she'd expected. "Can you elucidate why you asked your eldest daughter to, " he pulled down his pince-nez, reading from the transcript, "Cut off her big toe?" Dr. Brothers made the attempt to glance up from his scribbles.

"That arrogant young man. How dare he question me? Me the Lady Jewel!"

Constance, The Lady Jewel, blithely continued without catching the doctor's grim demeanor. She glared at his cardigan. *Brown.* More like a farmer. How could he judge her? She contended, "When the prince stopped by to find his mysterious princess I knew it had to be one of my beautiful daughters."

"But what does that have to do with your *own* daughter's severed toe?"

"The prince insisted. Yes! Insisted—as if I were a commoner—that my daughters pass a test. *She had to fit into a slipper.* Some dreadful thing left behind at the ball. It is all written down in your horrid *brown* file. Obviously."

"And that is relevant why?"

"Her foot was too big!" Oh he was an annoying little man. "My daughter may be beautiful, but she has no common sense. I told her all she had to do was *eliminate* her big toe. Problem solved, you see."

At this Dr. Brothers did look up. Pausing from his doodle, he inquired, "You see no problem with asking *your* daughter to cut off *her* toe?"

"You are an insipid little man. *Why* would she need a toe if she is married to the prince?"

Lady Jewel shifted in her chair craving nothing more than an end to this session. There was much to do and this brown man was clearly a waste of time. She had an appointment with her tailor. Her hair was not going to be styled on its own. And too, his smallness offended her.

"Tell me about the other incident. With your youngest daughter."

"That annoying prince. He claimed my eldest could not possibly be his princess. And, upon noticing the minimal amount, a trifling truly, of blood seeping out of the shoe..." The Lady's lacquered bejeweled hand addressed the brown file in Dr. Brother's lap. "He demanded I bring out another daughter!"

Was that judgment in his eyes? How dare he! Obviously he does not have beautiful daughters. "My youngest entered the room, curtsied, as any well bred ingénue of quality would. And, she *offered* to try on the slipper." Lady Jewel's breast rose and fluffed, hen-like. "Her delicate toes fit just fine—a relief. Her damnable *heel* would not slip in. So I..." At this she gave the tiniest of headshakes, side to side, as if erasing something from where it stuck in her mind.

Dr. Brothers wanted to be wrong, but braced himself for her answer. "You told her to cut off her heel?"

"Of course I did. What else was there to do? She did, as I demanded, being an obedient daughter. The shoe fit. End of story."

"Did she and the prince live happily ever after as is the law of our land?"

The Lady Jewell stared out the window at the castle on the hill. It was to have been her new home. She had already selected her suite of rooms.

"My inconsiderate daughter decided to bleed into the slipper just as her older sister had. So selfish. Neither of them thinks of me. So self-absorbed. Ungrateful."

Spilt Milk

The jailer led Lady Constance Jewel away. She had been granted her wish, a residence in the castle.

Just not the suite of rooms she'd planned for.

D.K. Cassidy

Octopus

The old Singer sewing machine hummed as the mother bent over her work. Depress the pedal. Sew two inches. Stop. Start again. She looked up at her children, huddled on the couch, the television blared the theme song from *The Brady Bunch*. Two skinny girls.

One of them stepped near her mother then stopped. No words exchanged, a waiting game, watching her creating the costume.

Finally, "Mommy, will it be ready in time?"

No answer.

The mother's right hand begins to hit the black-enameled metal. Over and over. In a trance-like state, she shatters the jade in her ring. Silence. Looking at her daughter, "Leave me alone. It'll be ready."

Dana returns to her sister, Faye. "I can tell, it'll be ready soon."

The two sisters exchange knowing glances. Dana didn't sit. Toward her mother, she spoke.

"The Halloween party's in two hours. Mommy will have my costume ready."

The sewing machine came to a stop. At the silence, Dana returned. Their mother stared at the costume. Again, the slamming came, her hand now on the sewing table. "Didn't—I—tell—you—leave me—alone."

Her free hand rose to rest on Dana's crown. Fingers closed around a clump of hair and yanked. Once. "Didn't I tell you to leave me alone?"

Dana refused to cry; her power was in not crying. She would not let anyone know she is hurt. She'd decided to be the protector by always drawing her mother's wrath from her sister. Biting her lower lip she stared with insolence.

This battle of wills lost, in resignation grasping fingers relaxed. Returning to her sewing chore. Stop. Go. Stop. Go.

After thirty minutes of them staring, she stood, tossing the costume to Dana.

Dana held it up to her sister, trying to figure it out. Faye raised her eyebrows. "I think it's an octopus." They giggled. Then after a quick glance back to the machine, they burst out laughing.

The octopus was plaid. The strangest costume the sisters had ever seen. At school they'd studied marine life and not one photo showed a plaid octopus. "Everyone already knows we're poor. If I wear this I won't be able to go back to school!"

The mother lay on her bed. Two Valium not helping, the only thing for it was a nap. Lights off. Shades drawn. Still. Quiet. Another migraine headache. She wouldn't get up for three days. Kim rolling over pushes thoughts of the day behind her. Her headaches always brought on recollections of her childhood, a lingering, unhappy memory of Korea. Drifting, she thought back about the journey that brought her here.

Time to head south and look for her uncle. She didn't have the luxury to wait for strength to return. Luxuries were a memory. Hundreds of miles left in Kim's trek. The South promised freedom from war. Dreams of abundant food. Safety and security. Her mother had promised it would. Kim, a princess child. Mornings a servant brought her a 'honey bucket' to relieve herself. Nothing in her earlier life trained her for this.

Kim heard a car pull up to her house. Too hollow to look out the window, she shifts in her bed, the pain rushes though the movement and pins her. Only the act of thinking moves her to return to her memories. Her migraine wins as she watches her younger self suffer.

The pungent odor of garlic and rice clinging to her tilted dark head, shadow obscuring her vacant face. Soldiers from Kaesong in the next room asking for more. "More rice! Hurry up. Don't forget our kimchee." A young Kim, the steaming bowls, bowing, apologizing. Not daring a look into anyone's eyes. Craving behind those

gaunt gazes. In the tiny kitchen, her small, chipped bowl.
Only one bowl allowed a day.

A timid knock on the door; her child disturbs
Kim's childhood. "Mommy? Mrs. Carry is
outside. I'm leaving now. Mommy?" Dana
backs gingerly away not wanting to be flattened
by a door flung in anger. No strength to answer
her daughter, drawing the shades used the last
remnant. Kim's eyes flutter then close, returning
to her reflections.

In the same place too long. If she started again, Kim's life
might change. She packs the few belongings she still
owns. Her mother's book. A sewing bundle. A few
tattered sheets of rice paper. Her Uncle's photo. His last
known address her chant as she walks. A real princess,
treated as one. Trained as an obedient girl. Her uncle's a
wealthy man.

From her nightstand a hidden bottle of soju
called to Kim. She relented, a gulp of wine will
ease the ache; boost the effect of the Valium,
too. The refrigerator and cabinets slapped open
and slammed shut, Faye crawling up on the

counters for food. The girls knew to respect the closed door. Fending for herself, knowing she's on her own for now.

Kim's back at that day her mother sent her away, saying *"Keep walking south."* And more. *"Avoid being swept up into the army."* *Maybe better than almost starving. Walking until her fragile body quivered. Not sure if she would ever see her Uncle and on some days, that little Kim didn't care. Her persistent wish a full belly and a safe, clean, bug free place to sleep.*

Nearing the release of sleep, she laid her head on the lump of her pillow. Smelling the familiar food of her distant home, mixing with thoughts of the last meal she'd shared with her mother and brother. Kim's hands covering her eyes to keep out the pain.

The men are always more important then a humble girl. Kim, pass the kimchee to your brother. Your brother gets the best and choicest bits of everything just like your father did when he was alive. Why aren't you eating? You think rice will be waiting for you every few feet as you travel to your Uncle's home? Do not disgrace me! Do not be an ungrateful girl!

The contestants of the Halloween contest circled the room, trying to catch the attention of the parents watching. A clown. A skeleton. A princess. A ghost. One costume stuck out, grabbing the attention of everyone in the room, a skinny girl's costume. A little plaid octopus.

Her head lowered, Dana followed the others in shame.

The judges conferred for a few moments. Reaching an accord, one stood to pronounce the winner. "You should all be proud. All of you have such great costumes. We've decided the winner this year, with the most creative and unusual costume…"

Dana's classmate had to nudge her; lost in dishonor, wishing the journey was over.

Dana ran into the house. Feeling rare. Excited. Happy. "Mommy! Mommy! Guess what? I won!" The sisters now knocked. Neither expecting an answer. Dana whispered once before turning. "Mommy I won."

Super Friends

"I'll have one dozen donuts. Picking up treats for the office. How about four maple bars, four cream filled with chocolate, they're called Bismarcks right? Do not know how I know that. Me? I never eat donuts. Let's make the final four apple fritters."

George tried to contain his excitement as the clerk filled the pink box; always-pink boxes it seemed, with delicious contents. A food orgasm, wave after wave, engulfed him as he watched each luscious bit of doughy goodness plop into the flat box. He disassociated for a moment, the shop became hazy around him and his vision swirled. He had to stop himself from grabbing at the hallucination circling just above the register.

After tossing money on the counter, not waiting for change, he rushed to his car, salivating. The first donut crammed in his mouth before the door opened. The second one he wolfed down as his seatbelt snapped, the third once he'd turned the ignition. Donuts four, five and six, inhaled within two miles. By the time he'd reached the next shop, a mere five miles later, George finished box one.

Checking his face in the rear view mirror for any telltale crumbs or frosting, brushing away evidence, George clumped into his next nirvana.

"I will have a dozen donuts. Picking up treats for the office. How about, umm, four maple bars, four cream filled with chocolate, they're called Bismarcks right? Do not know how I know that. Me? I never eat donuts. Let's make the final four apple fritters."

In his car George again munched on this latest dozen and thought about whether he wanted diet cola or chocolate milk with dinner. Diet cola won out. He made a third stop at the grocery store. He bought three 2-liter bottles, then waddled over to the deli.

"I will take four orders of General Tso's Chicken with fried rice. I'm having some people in later. Why don't you throw in a dozen fried pot stickers? And some extra sauce for that chicken."

He entered his first floor apartment, turning on the lights.

"Hello everyone, sorry to be late, had to make three stops tonight. Who wants a donut? Cola? Got some delicious General Tso's Chicken too."

Everyone remained silent.

"Really? No one? O.K. More for me." He bent down. "How about you kitty?"

George gave his hefty cat half of a pot sticker and watched his pet gobble the treat.

He settled on the couch and surveyed his friends: Captain America, Data, Aqua Man,

Captain Kirk, Iron Man, Captain Picard, and Wonder Woman. George pulled the coffee table closer.

At a younger age, his mother didn't want to let him out of the house; she didn't like her neighbors. Too busy showing off to take proper care of their children.

George became a computer programmer to please mother. The online course he passed gave him skills to earn a living but not ones to work in an office. The occasional freelance job was enough to pay the rent and feed him. George never wanted to be the object of her displeasure, never wanted to see her angry again.

Setting his culinary treasures in front of him, he smiled. He had such a diverse set of friends. No one accused him of being exclusive. He welcomed any and all who wanted to hang out.

In fact, he'd considered inviting Spock next. George held off hoping to invite Darth Vader, finding that Darth did not come in the size he preferred at his local friend store. His entire entourage had come from SuperFriends. George didn't like calling it a comic book store, like mother would. What he frequented definitely was a friend store. One of the few stores in which he could be himself and not what he thought people expected.

The cell phone rang disturbing his revelry; he knew it. Mother. Before even answering. No one else ever called. His group of friends didn't own phones. Her programs of choice, soap operas, televangelists, an occasional shopping channel, must have bored her. George braced himself for the onslaught he knew to expect. Taking a deep breath, as deep as he could manage, he answered.

"Mother. Hello. How are you?"

"You did not call me this morning. I could be lying on the floor dead. You wouldn't even know or care! You promised to call. Every morning and at least say hello. Why can't you do anything right? I need to depend on you. Didn't I always protect you from danger when you were a boy? Now I don't know what to do! I don't feel well, since noon, my heart is thumping, I feel faint…"

During her tirade, George continued to nod, stuffing food into his mouth, steady methodical movements matching the rhythm of her complaints. When his mother took a breath he jumped in with his usual reply.

"I forgot mother. And I am very sorry. This morning's—very busy, Things to do. A–a–nd forgot to call."

"You busy? You don't have a job, what would you do that kept you from calling your mother?"

"You seem OK, right mother? I promise to call. Tomorrow morning. I'll even write a note and stick it on the refrigerator. Won't forget. Will that be OK?"

After his mother hung up, George felt hungry all over again. Time to look for his next meal. It had been a long time, at least a week, since he'd gotten Italian food. He remembered the hours for his favorite restaurant, calling in his order.

"Yes, I am having a small gathering at my home this evening. I would like to order lasagna with sausage. Cannelloni. Umm, two orders of your special ravioli. One Caesar salad without chicken; one of my friends is a vegetarian. Four orders of garlic bread, and a pint—no make it two pints of spumoni ice cream. Thank you." He smiled, promising to be there in minutes.

Turning to his friends. George told them all he'd be back and not to tear up the place or leave before he returned.

They all stared at him in mute agreement. Intelligence and kindness in their stares. No one would misbehave. George lumbered out the door and wedged himself into his car. Backing out of the driveway, he cursed himself for not bringing a snack. He feared he might get hungry on the trip.

His Italian food on the coffee table, the only place he ate anymore, George flipped on the television, and found something to distract him for the evening. His mother's favorite reality show about losing weight was not on tonight. He settled for watching a program about the best places to eat ice cream.

Someday he'd like to go on a road trip and visit every one of those shops. He couldn't imagine a better way to spend his time. Unless of course he could visit the best All You Can Eat Buffets around the country. Then again, George would be too self-conscious to eat in front of anyone other than the friends who lived with him. These friends had never called him fat. Or worthless. Or freak.

Mother thought he'd build character if she constantly told him about his shortcomings. It was kinder, coming from someone who loved you.

At midnight George turned on his computer and began to play THE game. The one that let everyone role-play. You could be anyone you wanted. No one knew what you looked like. This activity was his favorite. Well, his favorite was eating, but gaming definitely stood a close second.

He logged on: Blue Freund, his character's name, and looked for a group to join. His character a tall, thin, blonde elf with powers to use magic spells. Blue Freund yielded a powerful staff.

The battle about to begin and his request to join accepted. George had just enough time to stock the area around his computer; battle always made him hungry and thirsts must be quenched. His kitty and his silent friends looked on as George slew his enemies and looted their dead corpses.

Despite what Mother had said, the night was going to be a great.

D.K. Cassidy

Spilt Milk

Caleb's father started the day as usual. As he always did, ignoring his son. At breakfast he downed his coffee. Mixed with whiskey. Inhaled his cigarette, and watched TV. Caleb made his own breakfast, fake Coco Puffs doused with chocolate milk. It didn't take much; spilled cereal scattered on the floor set off his father. Any excuse for punishing his son.

"Idiot!" his father yelled, "Stupid moron." This litany was a morning beat Caleb knew well.

Tradition. Reaching over, he punched Caleb.

"Clean it boy." His father kicked him with each word, punctuating his threat, "or you'll really be hurting." Caleb scooped up the cereal, put it in the garbage. He understood his job.

Paralyzed, he stood outside himself as he got to it. The kitchen became cold and Caleb's vision whitened. His heart sped up until it might explode and take him out of his misery. He shivered waiting for that merciful moment. Caleb floated, leaving his body to his dad, morphing, disinterested in what might happen next. With no place in him to ignore his father, his shaking intensified.

Caleb observed himself glance at the wooden block on the counter. He stared at his hand as it grabbed a shiny steel blade. His reflection unrecognizable; eyes empty, cold, expressionless. All emotion extracted there. Walking up behind his father, Caleb now stands. Waiting.

The sound blaring off the TV completes the weird moment. A local news story about happy families celebrating great fathers.

His shaking stopped; he became calm. Caleb saw himself almost do it. He's taking a breath. He's held it. Without intention he's nodding three times.

The knife plunging into his dad's neck, surprised to feel the slit reached all the way around. Squirting blood formed a graceful arc over the kitchen table, just missing Caleb's bowl, empty of cereal.

Dead in seconds, Caleb didn't feel finished. He took to the next job.

Caleb talked to his father.

"Hate you." He said. Using the knife. "See your blood in my bowl? I'm not cleaning up this mess. Hate you." Ignoring the blood as he sawed. "See your finger in the ashtray? I'm gonna make the biggest mess you've ever seen, you idiot!"

He wondered as the TV droned, *would they say things about him?* Not on the news, that'd be boring. On one show some celebrity had given birth to a baby boy. She declared her love, naming him something unique and unpronounceable. Then the World Series was on. Caleb kept on with his job. Then contestants on a singing show, trying for reality in the final week.

Nobody cared about an unimportant murder.

His task was complete. But it was another two hours until he picked up the telephone dialing 911, to inform the dispatcher about his deed. Hanging up, Caleb pulls his bowl of cereal nearer.

DKC

She dreamt she was a mermaid. Not the fairy-tale type, instead a proud mythical creature. Swimming the ocean free from the limits of gravity or dread.

Once, a stranger shot Naiad. At the trial he testified; he'd tried to slay his ex-girlfriend. Wearing her hair in just the right way, dressed as he remembered her, at his conviction he professed Naiad 'had to be the one'. He pleaded. "Recognize me." The guard dragged him from the courtroom. A photo appeared in the local paper. It's true, it could be her.

Wade, her physical therapist, promised to help her heal. Naiad's prospects for walking impossible, she became a brave-faced cripple. Yes, she called herself a cripple but didn't give anyone else permission. It wouldn't be right, wouldn't be kind. It wouldn't make one feel virtuous. But Naiad loved to label herself *cripple*. To wallow in her private self-pity, then put on an opaque public face when on land.

Naiad's innocent family assumed a fancy wheelchair made her malformed self feel normal. Not the prior normal. Nothing could be normal again. Time to create a novel reality. Time for Naiad to become a mermaid.

The therapy pool, warm and shallow, full of bobbing white-haired wonders appreciative to be breathing. Naiad dropped into the pool via a lift, that's how all cripples entered the pool. Feeling sympathetic eyes of the old women shame her. She wants to shout, 'Don't look, don't feel sorry, leave me alone!'

Hating attention, she closed her eyes until the chlorinated warmth enveloped her body. Her being drinking in the peace of floating. Aloft. Naiad became an abled woman again. The 'dis' abandoned on the pool's deck. Refusing to acknowledge her nemesis waiting staunchly by the lifeguard, her new body turns away.

Her folks named her Naiad. Water nymph. Her fanciful parents admirers of mythology. Naiad not so much. She did not have long flowing hair, and up until now, loathed the water. Never dreamt of swimming. The dream of an offspring with the attributes of a water nymph evaporated the first time her daughter jumped into a pool. Mother and toddler swim lessons a disaster. Her little water nymph screamed, until the instructor advised them to leave. Too late to change her name.

Today's session floating on her back. Nailed it. She'd expected more; Wade didn't want to tire her out. Time to go home.

I'm 28 not 82! How can I tell him the water's my habitat? My lover.

Naiad floated, lost in the warm embrace of each atom of water. Millions holding her mangled body enfolded in their balminess, allowing her to remember euphoria. Her true self left behind in the pool, hoisted to the patient 'dis'.

Three days before she could feel joy once again.

Her chariot waits to ferry Naiad home. The ancient driver acknowledges his charge, offering assistance into the empty van.

"Where to little minnow?" he burbles as if he'd never asked before.

"To my seaside castle, kind sir," the customary reply in this game. Niceties over, brave face planted.

Naiad never noticed the walkers before, now she grew obsessed with the different varieties of gait, speed, whatever variances the entitled used. Her eyes fixated on the dull ones. They all took for granted the magic of legs. Does she envy them their supple limbs? Of course.

No roommate, no paid helper, just Naiad. Her arms work. She can do for herself and pines for the privacy. This cripple wants to wipe herself in peace. Bed low to the floor, easy to roll over and enter the sanctuary of her dreams. Painless to leave this life behind and find her genuine one. Or no life at all.

Swimming closer to the island searching for someone. Knowing there's a man there she needs to see. Approaching the shore Naiad notices a small cottage. Standing in the doorway a child. She waves then runs inside. The surrounding water is turbulent, full of life.

Fish? Diving to explore, to feel the liberation of movement. The ecstasy of moving her lower half. Legs melding into a green tail of iridescent scales. Naiad's tale.

This time she told Wade she needed to do more in the pool. He adds turning over from a floating position. Before he can end the session, stretching her arms, Naiad begins to swim. She pulls the warm water towards her. Ten stokes and she's won, turning to see Wade admiring her daring and progress. Muscles on her slack face form an atrophied smile. She'd forgotten that feeling.

Fresh van driver today. Not so old. Not nearly so chatty. Naiad's facade drops. His name, George, hand printed in enormous block letters on his nametag. Naiad wonders why he'd want this job. They pull up to the castle; George lets out a grunt, signals their arrival.

Morbidly obese. Not moving to assist, George

looks as if he could use her help. She backs down the ramp and notices a doll on the chariot's dashboard. Wonder Woman. If only.

During this morning's session Naiad begs to swim underwater but Wade thinks she's not ready. Time to show him how ready she is. Investigating the bottom of the pool, weightless, silence listens to her heart. Naiad's seaweed hair hovers, framing her pale face.

Every corner of the pool now part of this woman's sovereignty. Breaking the surface she realizes water is her element. Princess Naiad bequeaths air, fire, and earth to walkers. She chooses water.

Agua, eau, mizu,
wasser, mool, ama.

Language isn't a province; it is all her domain.

Another evening alone by choice. The end of each day finds her exhausted from pretending. Each day, plastering a brave face on the real Naiad takes more effort. Temptation to stop growing stronger, reasons to keep feigning happiness; falling in scales from her.

Flawless blue water, warmed by sun. Naiad swims up, breaching the surface tension. In the distance the lone man and child stare. They jump into the water and swim towards the princess. The ocean welcoming them, drawing them home. Flipping her tail she dives.

Decaf or Regular?

ecaf or regular? Wait…I think I'm supposed to say regular first. Shit! OK, what did she say about size? Jared Teabottom was the only one not paying attention.

Writing at the front of the class, Corinne Cockcrow stood at the whiteboard, scribbling out the new baristas script. Her pupils studied the information like scripture. The rules were exact, no room for interpretation. Jared focused solely on coveting Ms. Cockcrow's ass. At that moment he decided to become her best student.

Three months earlier Jared was drifting. No ambition. No relationship. No belief. An empty vessel ready for filling. One fateful day he found Celestial Coffee. Walking up to the barista he ordered. It changed the course of his life.

"Regular or decaf? Small, Medium, Large? For here or to go? Room for cream?" chirped the perky acolyte.

"Um…just a cup of coffee."

"Yes, but we at Celestial Coffee want to make your coffee experience perfect. How about a Grande?" *Coffee experience?* He wondered how she said that without laughing. Jared felt jolted by the menu's prices. *How about robbery.* "You know what? I'll have the smallest you got. Forgot the ATM." He nearly genuflected, "Only have two bucks."

The barista looking upon him, sympathetic, leaned closer and whispered, "This one's on me. All you have to do is come back and say *hi*."

It took Jared a week to work up the nerve to visit again. He pushed open the glass and chrome door with purpose. Walked in, then backed out immediately. Why was he here? The coffee they offered wasn't *that good, tasted too burnt.* Besides, she didn't even look legal. What was pulling him? Getting laid wasn't the issue. He walked down the street, turned. Something drew Jared back. On the door hung a sign, it spoke to him: *Hiring, inquire within.*

Corinne Cockcrow had moved on, sermonizing now on the coffee paraphernalia part of Sunday's class. Arrayed on a large silver tray, atop a table draped in dark heavy cloth, lay the instruments of the barista. They glittered in the fluorescent light, calling to Jared. He handled each piece with reverence, pausing to feel. A litany rose in him, *Porta-filter, Group Head, Burr Grinder, Doser—and, and— damn, I'm too dense to* remember. Jared turned to see Corinne eyeing him, the lone male sparrow.

Never good at public speaking, his voice quivered, standing in front of the class. Trying to define the items they'd just been chanting. Sweat in places both embarrassing and surprising. "Group Head—where the employees go the bathroom," He heard giggling. "Porta-filter—used in the bathroom to separate—"

Realized belatedly he'd been speaking aloud.
Head down he rushed to his seat.

If Jared couldn't recite something, he resorted
to humor. Time to show Corinne Cockcrow and
Celestial Coffee, he was worthy. He could
transcend the expectation of his peers, his
parents, beyond the class cut-up. Time to
change that perception.

He'd taken two buses from his studio
apartment. The interview at a huge warehouse.
Jared ran his shaking hands through his curly
hair, trying to dry his palms. Facing this
corporate headquarters in the industrial section
of Seattle.

The smell of fresh ground beans hit his nose.
His salivary glands went wild. In the lobby stood
a massive chrome espresso machine. Arrayed
around the table lay bags of coffee, left as
offerings to the idol. These people were serious

about caffeine. Spotlights aimed at the machine blinded him momentarily. Jared felt the need to whisper, to genuflect. Rooted to the floor, he wiped his open mouth of drool.

Jared planned studying the next section of the employee manual all weekend long, Sunday especially. In the bathroom, he noticed the small print: *Only for use by employees of Celestial Coffee.* Leaning prayer-fashion to read it, *Anyone else found with this manual will be executed.* Umm. A bit intense. Was this a typo? Some HR person's last *fuck you.* What kind of a group was this? Was this for real?

He settled in to learn about Cupping.

A row of white porcelain cups set up by Corinne Cockcrow waited on the table. Each filled. Today the apprentices would be learning to check the taste of coffee. *Aroma, Sweetness, Flavor, Acidity, Cleanness, I've got this. Body, Balance, Aftertaste. I'm worthy, I'm worthy, I'm gonna nail this.*

After tasting all twelve varieties Jared had still failed to notice the waiting spittoon. He had noted three things: The taste was all-same. His hands kept shaking. His bladder was bursting. No break for 30 minutes. Could he wait that long?

Brilliant. Always sitting in the back of the room was going to pay off. An empty coffee sack lay in the wastebasket next to him.

He coughed while unzipping. Sighed. Shivered. Smiled.

After four weeks of intensive indoctrination, the apprentices, ready to proselytize about Celestial Coffee, were released to an unsuspecting flock.

"Regular of decaf? Small, Medium, Large? For here or to go? Room for cream?" chirped a jerky Jared. Adjusting his crisp black barista's apron with pride, as the wary customer before him stood debating.

"Um…just a cup of coffee."

"Yes, but we at Celestial Coffee want to make your coffee experience perfect. How about a Grande?" Jared parroted without laughing.

The customer looked at the jam jar on the counter, *Tip Karma*. Jared waited.

D.K. Cassidy

Birthday Boy

For eight years Caleb waited for this day. Patience not being one of his strong points; it could be said Caleb lacked any virtues. To make the time pass faster he watched T.V., played video games, and read. Making friends in this crazy place? No interest. Keeping to himself, his usual way, became an easy decision.

Caleb's guardian ad litem had convinced him being in a mental hospital would be far easier, and a much better choice, than juvenile detention. After the first few nights of patients screaming Caleb didn't agree. His plea deal, incarceration, along with years of counseling and medication. Set in stone. Not changeable. He waited petulantly for his release at eighteen.

The psychiatrist treating Caleb enquired about the first time he'd killed anything. The doctor re-reads his notes, trying to understand what led to the gruesome murder. All these years later, as if the file's contents would change. Right from the start, Caleb told the man what he wanted to hear while watching the doctor scribble in his notebook. Claiming no memory of harming anyone or anything. But Caleb remembered the truth.

The third and final stone on the frog. Sitting back, bored. Hop. Hop. Nothing else. A rainy afternoon. Watching the green flatten and ooze into the mud. The smell of the mud reminding him of burnt toast. That slimy thing disappointed him. It didn't make a noise, not even a croak, so he'd stood up on stout, dimpled legs, and hopped into his house. Bored. Not bothering with a backward glance, giggling about the dead froggy. Entering the dark house. Yelling, "Daddy!" Till he'd found him.

"Were you playing in the mud? You're a filthy mess."

"I'm hungry, want a samich"

"I don't feed pigs!" screamed his father.

Spilt Milk

"Hungry, hungry, hungry!!!! Wanna samich!"

His father slapped him. Told him to wash up. But Caleb just stared, keeping the tears in his brimming eyes from spilling over. Warm urine trickling down his legs.

"Hate you! Hate you."

His father ignored the outburst; he'd turned away pouring himself another cupful.

His session with the psychiatrist finished, Caleb waited out the last few hours in the common room, writing. He'd begun a journal when he first entered the facility, keeping track of his chaotic thoughts and rants.

White walls, so damn depressing. I think these damn walls will wear me out. I grew up in a white house, but the walls weren't white. I've always wanted yellow walls. My bedroom was painted blue. Grandmother said they'd clash. Blue walls are depressing too. As if I care about that. I never made my bed; I couldn't see the sense in it. My bed just got messed up again at night.

Caleb stared at the common room clock willing the hands to fly. He tapped his fingers to a song only he heard. His left leg in constant motion, a metronome. A tooth-marked ballpoint pen in his mouth.

What a shitty way to celebrate turning 18, glaring at white walls. At least I think it's my birthday. It might be the 28th—isn't it? My phone says it is, it must be so. Why does everyone else trust machines? I'm suspicious of all machines except for my phone. They don't seem to like me. Before I got to this damned place, irons burnt my pants, washers ate my socks; machines hate me. Now the candy machines steal my coins. Cheap hospital. Won't give me candy— have to buy my own. Orderlies and crazies sneak into my room. Steal it! Machines and people stealing from me. His pen flew along the page.

He jumped off his place on the couch. Checked his phone, his lifeline. Making friends wasn't a skill in his family. His grandmother only wanted to spend time with Caleb, her son, and the 4 cats patrolling the house. There used to be 5 cats. Caleb took an interest in the calico, one dark afternoon.

Used to be, I couldn't wait for my birthday. He wrote, once he could settle again, No one came but grandmother, my father, and my latest 'mom'. I didn't care; all I wanted were the presents. Grandmother gave me a party every year until that year. Then the parties stopped; nothing to look forward to. Why am I still here? I'm dying to see something other than these damn walls.

He remembered his grandmother speaking to the cats more than anyone else. No hugs, just hits. No conversation, just nods. Or grunts. Something changed. Caleb's her last living relative.

He killed his father 8 years ago. But he didn't write that down.

This would be the best birthday ever because he planned everything himself. Caleb knew what he wanted. He would make it happen. Another check of his phone before he gets to celebrate his birthday.

At 4pm, the orderly escorted Caleb to the office. The guardian ad litem sat waiting for Caleb's discharge papers, no longer his problem, or the state's. Caleb's left leg resumed its metronome beat. He signed with his favorite pen then bolted to the exit, leaving his early days in the dust.

Caleb stepped off the bus. Walked the last few blocks to his childhood home. Now it belonged to him, memories included. He sat in the recliner staring out at the backyard. A jungle of weeds and neglect looked back. Dust coated every surface, laying claim to the abandoned house. Caleb didn't care, it was all his. Time to start his birthday party.

His father's blue Toyota in the driveway of his white house, waiting for his special day to begin. He turned the ignition, surprised to hear it growl, adjusted the rearview mirror, backing out leisurely. His iPod blared one of his favorite tunes as he headed toward the freeway.

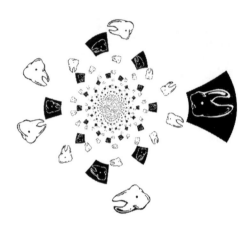

His childhood treasures remained up in his mother's attic. His current obsession bored him. It had been years since George started a new collection. Time to move on.

Six months ago George drove a van, picking up disabled passengers. It was nice, he guessed. He didn't need to talk to anybody. Yet he couldn't stand the boredom of driving all day. There was one woman who intrigued him, but George was far too shy to engage her in any way. He never talked, why start now? Besides, one day she stopped coming to the pool; he never saw her again. He quit soon after that.

Surfing the Internet, not sure what he was looking for, he visited various websites to pass the time. George found an article about parenting. He knew he'd never become a dad, not for lack of desire. No woman would let him do *that* to her. Through the evening he surfed. Nothing pleased. Nothing held him. George had enough of passing the time. No social life, no girlfriend, no way to pass the interminable empty hours in his day. He reached to shut down his PC, when one word jumped from the screen, implanting itself in George's brain.

Tooth.

Nurse Wendy kept a box of 1"X 2" manila envelopes. Storing lost molars, canines, and bicuspids of her students, was her service to parents. The nurse kept asking George about missing envelopes. George wasn't a suspect; he was a good employee of Midlands Elementary School. Being the custodian just made him the logical person to ask.

You wouldn't imagine the things George had turned over to the office since he'd started. Yet, every week at least one teary, gap-smiled child told Nurse Wendy they couldn't find their treasure.

Still, he felt nervous about the attention. George needed to find another supply. It became more difficult for him, getting teeth.

Changing his daily cleaning routine, George started avoiding the nurse's office. He picked up a School District jobs listing, on the way to the bakery.

He scrolled through ads on Craigslist, noticing an interesting post after a few minutes of browsing. George read it aloud, "No Experience Required. Willing to Work at Night. Must Like Salvaging."

That described him. George had a computer programming degree, but didn't like showing up at an office. Hated sharing his personal space with others. He clicked on the 'Reply' icon to inquire about the position's particulars.

His email answered in moments. George wondered if the person on the other side stayed camped by his monitor hoping for someone.

Reading out loud again, made George feel his luck was genuine. More solid. "Your qualifications seem perfect for the position. I will pay a finders fee for any items I deem worthy for my use. Please meet me Friday evening behind Hillcrest Medical Center. Bring latex gloves and dress in dark clothing. I look forward to our joint venture. Regards, Caleb"

Caleb was waiting by the medical waste dumpster, an excited grin spread across his thin pale face. George's extended hand rebuffed, "Sorry, I don't touch living people."

Without a word, gloved and ready, the pair dove into the treasure box of red Biohazard bags. Meant to be incinerated in the morning, this waste material from doctors and dentists offices. George began to feel a chill run up his spine, a good chill, something close to happiness. They were compatible collectors. Caleb wanted femurs for making flutes; George wanted more teeth for…he wasn't sure.

Entering his dark apartment, George looked to the half empty bookshelf. He felt the shelves needed more decorations. He placed tonight's haul next to its current occupants. Until now, everything had been rather small. Now George had larger items to display next to their miniature versions. His collection was getting diverse.

The muscles on his face trembled then formed his version of a grin.

The third time they met, George worked up the nerve to ask Caleb why he was drawn to making flutes. Caleb's reply, the longest conversation they would ever have, commenced, "I read the Neanderthals made flutes from the femur of bears. I decided to experiment on other bones. Human bones have the loveliest tone and the best tasting marrow."

"Mother, why are you throwing away my friends?"

"You are a grown man. Grown men do not play with DOLLS!"

George began to see his mother's therapist soon after the disposal of his friends. Tired of being alone, wanting to lead a normal life, he sought the help of Dr. Tine, after lunch with mother one Friday. Always one to interfere, his mother slipped one of her Xanax into George's milkshake. Relax him a bit.

Spilt Milk

This psychiatrist understood George. He dispensed with the usual questions and asked George about nightmares.

"It's this same dream two months now. It just won't go 'way. I wake up in a sweat and hot. Like it's happening to me. I'm walking down my old street. It's night. All alone not scared or nervous. Just looking around and thinking, *why am I on this street at night?* Feels pretty late. Maybe one or two in the morning. My mother's house is on this—the street; it's dark and— very still. I think, *that's strange.* 'cause she leaves the porch light on when I'm out. I look. And think, that's *kind of strange.* Then I think I see some *thing.* It *moves.* Up in the attic."

George pauses to take a breath. His sentences came in monosyllables, not narratives. Dr. Tine shifted in his seat, never taking his eyes away. From where George sat he could almost count the Doctor's front teeth. George stops again to wipe the sweat from his upper lip.

George sits in the darkest corner of the pub watching the Irish fiddler set up his music stand. He's dropped mother off. She was angry at his terseness this last time. Now he sips his Guinness as he has for the previous three Fridays. Maybe therapy was working.

George shifted on his barstool to reach into his pants pocket. Fondling his treasures, deciding what to do with his cache. He jerks his hand away looking around to see if anyone noticed. The musician starts to play, the crowd expectant. Georges scans the couples, reminding him of the emptiness in his gut. His hand returns to his pocket caressing his enamel nuggets of joy.

The lights come up, old and new friends float away. George moves past these couplings longing to be one of them. He boards a bus headed to where? Home was no longer a description of his apartment. It was a place to sleep, play games, and pass the time. His friends evicted last year.

The drill bit worked quite well. A 1mm hole bored in the lateral side allowed the string through. His collection totaled thirty-two, the average number for most people.

Drill, string, tie a knot, repeat. The glittering enamel necklace ready just in time for Mother's Day. The Doctor helped so much. And Caleb can show him how that flute sounds.

D.K. Cassidy

Invisible Joy

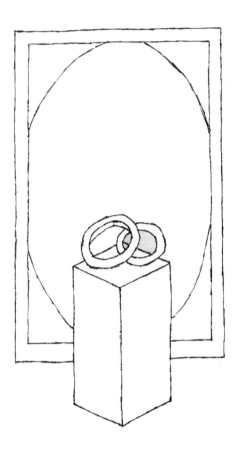

*C*ouldn't night take over and leave the day to those who deserved it? *Why does morning always arrive?* She stretched, hitting the snooze button again. *Who thought they deserved to leap out of bed, and* 'seize the day'? *God, that's such a stupid saying.* The muslin light filtering in through the curtains continued pissing her off.

Groping for her cigarettes with closed eyes, Joy expertly lit a smoke, rolling over in one smooth motion. Unable to delay any longer, she sat up. Yesterday's coffee sat in the mug. *All right.* It'd just needed one minute in the microwave to be drinkable.

She brushes her hair automatically; it gleams with the oils from her filthy scalp. Although still early, Joy feels fatigued. Anxiety a constant companion whining for attention, while she contemplates her slippers.

Now for the mental list of things not to do today: Panic. Feel regret. Drink any alcohol. Take more than 2 naps. Things not to forget: Car keys. Feed cats. Take shower. Xanax, renew my prescription.

The crust on the cat food just needed to be stirred a bit. *All right.* The litter box out of sight; smell tolerable. Deal with it later. There were things to lay out. Things to let go to Goodwill. *How exhausting.* The recliner beckoned, fifteen feet to her chair. She counted it as her daily exercise. *All right.* At least she moved, didn't that count?

In two weeks. Fifty. At least that's what her birth certificate said. In her mind her early twenties held sway; still beautiful and desired. When did that change? Passing a mirror, even if she squinted, all Joy saw was some stranger. Nothing particularly glamorous or exciting, a spreading matron.

This bra feels tight. Could it be shrinking? I should buy an extender, till I start loosing weight. Maybe take ice cream off the list? Then how will I get through the night? Why did that man bump into me? What am I, invisible? Is wine better than ice cream?

Juggling bags from the pharmacy, pet store, and grocer, Joy felt like a circus act not worth paying for. Wild hair and baggy pants might let her pass for a clown. *Damit.* Her car sat wedged between two huge SUVs. In anticipation of the squeeze she held in her stomach, breathless. A numb thumb and finger finally easing the key into place.

Cleaning the car never makes it on her list of things not to forget. Eating a hotdog while backing out of a parking space was perfected after trading in the stick shift for an automatic. Joy felt at home in her car. *Trash filled, so what.* Toss it over your shoulder, it disappears. Forgotten.

At a red light Joy glances to her right at a blue Toyota. Inside a man in his teens texting. His concentration intense, the world outside the 4-inch screen non-existent. At one point in her life she'd known that kind of intensity; it had been directed at her. At that moment, he looked over, moving his gaze past the outline of her vehicle, never meeting her eyes. Looking through her.

Her stubby icicle fingers clutched the steering wheel the rest of the way home.

Was it already ten years since her second husband? She wasn't sure how he did it, but thought perhaps he just willed his heart to stop. She knew he'd wanted to die. An avid runner, a healthy eater, the only thing remotely stressful to him was Joy.

Every time she opened her mouth Joy had a way of making him annoyed. He'd say, *I buy you something, you lose interest.* He always griped, *Nothing's good enough or expensive enough for you.* Her appetite never sated. She didn't know if it ever would be. *On to the next thing.*

For Joy it somehow made her feel better to place the blame on him. Like tossing a hot dog wrapper behind her. Age had not given her any sense of perspective or sense. Underneath the frumpy exterior, lived the shallow, conceited woman she once was and always would be.

As long as she avoided mirrors, she could remember herself as the beauty just out of nursing school. Ready to take on the world and any man who looked at her. Her confidence was always her best asset.

As she pulled into her driveway, Joy remembers her lists of things today. *All right*. She'd feed her cats and call her lists complete. The shower would wait. The Xanax would keep her serene. A glass of wine after the parking lot. If she didn't drink, she would feel regret. She did need beauty sleep. *Of course*, a nap.

Joy unlocked her door, adjusting her eyes to dimness. She must have flipped off the lights when she'd left. The tall trees in her yard always made her house seem dark, another thing she hated about this place.

Her old nurse's uniform draped over her recliner, inviting her to sit. White shoes and stockings were there as well, to complete her ensemble. Yes, it would all go. On the TV tray that tubing. So familiar. She'd quit being a nurse thanks to her husband. Beneath her to nurse now. Her eyes drawn back to the tubing.

The front door slammed. Joy recognized that staring man, the one who'd ignored her. Familiar. The guy texting on his phone. Without eye contact, he'd looked over her. Around her. Never at her.

Not panicking, Joy continued to stare. His right hand draped in surgical tubing. Why was he here? Why didn't he speak to her? *Who'd sent him?* Joy backed away. He matched her step for step until she felt the far wall of her living room with her cold, cold fingertips.

At last he made eye contact while humming the birthday song.

J *ust one more. OK another one.* Pria couldn't help herself. *Well if I pluck one more on each side they'll be even.* She loved to pluck her eyebrows every other Sunday.

On Mondays, Pria plucked her guitar for exactly twenty-five minutes. No particular tune. She couldn't read music. Plucking the strings one at a time.

E, A, D, G, B, E.

Tuesdays were for plucking up her courage to try new things. This week: riding the bus across town alone. She plucked exact change out of her purse. The bus driver stared; she saw that, perhaps he was fascinated by her skill. Pluck, pluck, plucking up courage.

Wednesday, oh Wednesday, her favorite plucking day of all. Pria went to Central Park to pluck pigeons. The covetous birds loved the crumbs of cornbread she used to lure them. Closer they ventured, greedily pecking at the morsels of golden goodness. Pria only plucked two feathers from each plump bird. It was perfect. Once she'd acquired twenty-one feathers she stopped. Seven goes into twenty-one three times.

On Pria's non-plucking Sundays she rested. Eyebrows required the time to grow. Plucked cuticles needed to repair themselves. Her busy brain wanted to reset for another week of plucking.

Thursday, Friday, and Saturday were workdays for her. The pickle factory. Her job was quality assurance, she never called it QA. As the thousands of pickles flew past on the conveyor belt, Pria paid, yes paid, to pluck bad pickles and toss them into a bin behind her. She relished her job.

Her days at work were planned so she seemed to fit in. Chatting with co-workers, yet never going out with them. *They pluck so unmercifully at people they laughed at.* Seldom reaching for her eyebrows in front of others. Didn't want to be ridiculed. Her brain trying to manage busy fingers. Reading a book, turning the pages in a smooth open-handed motion. Ignoring the itchy twitching in her mind. Being someone else to survive.

Reaching for her time card last Thursday, her supervisor gave her a pink slip. Pria decided not to panic. She plucked it out of his outstretched hand using her public smile.

Entering her apartment, Pria carried on. Plucking calendar pages, surveying ways to track the passage of time. Washing a handful of grapes, setting them aside. She would take care of them later. No time to enjoy them now. The room began to spin, her head pounded, her fingers grasping then plucking at her lips.

Rising from the floor she resolves to find a new job. Pria enjoys the fruit, plucking one dark orb at a time from its stem, planning her new life. Pulling grapes, the quiet snap relaxing her. The rhythm of her fingers reassuring.

The morning paper gifted her a job. She spotted the tiny ad on the bottom of page pigeon. *Pigeon*, Pria's name for twenty-one.

"Florist assistant. Thursday through Saturday. No experience required. Must be available immediately," she breathed softly, luring the job closer, it seemed.

"Have you ever done any gardening? Deadheaded flowers? Can you work 6am-2pm? Can you start tomorrow?" The florist's rapid questions continued for another three minutes. Stopping, he peered at Pria over his half-moon glasses. She nodded yes. Yes to it all. The deal done. For once he wouldn't have to deal with a chatterer.

Fired after one week. Pria couldn't stop deadheading the faded blooms. She plucked and plucked until all the flowers were bald. Ruining the blooms not the goal but rather the outcome. Once she started, her fingers wouldn't let her stop. Her trip home on the bus allowed a time for reflection. Pria's left hand crept up to her eyebrows.

Picking fruit, her next endeavor, lasted three days. Stock clerk, seven. Dog walker lasted pigeon days. Somehow, the owners found out she'd tied the dogs to a tree in Central Park. Visiting her pigeon friends, instead of exercising their precious pets.

Refusing to become despondent, Pria used her bus rides to make new resolutions. Her left hand remaining motionless in her lap.

Never using her fireplace, she decided this was the day to christen it. She placed her feathers in a pile on the floor. With the guitar set on her lap she cut the strings, listening to twangs of pity. She didn't need wood to build a healthy fire, her guitar worked well. The feathers sizzled rather than burned. Her pluckers held over the flames for a count of pigeon. *Goodbye cuticles*. The cleansing flames healed her.

A pleased Pria stared at her bandaged hands, dreaming at last of a future without plucking.

Acknowledgments

To Arlene V., Barb B., Jean T., Ken T., and Michelle B. I am grateful for your support. I could not have written this without the nudges and encouragement from each of you. My dream is now reality.

To EJ my patient editor, thank you for helping me see the golden bits buried in piles of garbage.

About the Author

D.K. Cassidy has been scribbling stories since she was a child and loves to write in various genres including Magical Realism, Urban Gothic, Science Fiction, and Literary Fiction.

Her goal? Messing with your mind by transforming the voices in her head into odd stories.

D.K. Cassidy lives in the Pacific Northwest with her greatest fans: her husband Mark, twin sons Aidan and Jared, and three cats. When not writing, she loves to travel, run, use the Oxford comma, and of course read!

If you like her work please follow her:
@moongie
http://www.dkcassidy.com/
www.facebook.com/DKCassidyAuthor

35498377R00069

Made in the USA
San Bernardino, CA
25 June 2016